# HUFF and PUFF'S APRIL SHOWERS

Illustrated by Molly Piper
Activity Illustrations by Marion Hopping Ekberg

Totline® Publications, P. O. Box 2250, Everett, WA 98203

Printed in Hong Kong through Phoenix Offset.
First Edition 10 9 8 7 6 5 4 3 2

Warren, Jean, 1940-
    Huff and Puff's April Showers / by Jean Warren ; illustrated by Molly Piper ; activity illustrations by Marion Ekberg.
       p.       cm.
    Summary: Cloud children Huff and Puff grieve over losing the money they had hoped to spend for a Mother's Day present, but their tears water the flowers and help create a special present. Includes crafts and other activities.

    ISBN 0-911019-78-2 : $5.95

    (1. Clouds—Fiction. 2. Mother's Day—Fiction. 3. Gifts—Fiction. 4. Stories in rhyme.)
I. Piper, Molly, 1949- ill. II. Ekberg, Marion Hopping, ill. III. Title.
PZ8.3.W2459Hw 1994
(E)—dc20
                                            93-5489
                                          CIP
                                          AC

Totline® Publications would like to acknowedge the following activity contributors:

Diane Thom, Maple Valley, WA
Becky Valenick, Rockford, IL
Kristine Wagoner, Puyallup, WA
Saundra Winnett, Fort Worth, TX
Angela Wolfe, Miamisburg, OH

# HUFF and PUFF'S
# APRIL SHOWERS

**Warren Publishing House**

Once upon an April day,
Huff and Puff were heard to say,
"We need to work so we can pay
For a gift on Mother's Day!"

So off they went
To try and find
Jobs of almost any kind.

They watered lawns
And gardens, too.
They rinsed off animals
At the zoo.

At last their pockets
Were full of pay,
Enough for a present
On Mother's Day.

Up, up they floated
In the sky,
Dreaming of gifts
That they could buy.

Perhaps a rainbow
For Mother's hair,
Perhaps a brand-new
Rocking chair.

They floated on
Without a care,
Until they crashed—
In midair!

They lost their balance,
They lost their pay,
Down, down it fell
Into a bay.

"Our money's gone,
What can we do?
Sniff, sniff, sniff,
Boo-hoo, boo-hoo."

They cried and cried
For hours and hours,
Filling the skies with
April showers.

All the way home,
Wherever they flew,
They showered the towns
And the people too.

At last came the day
For Mother in May,
And Huff and Puff
Were sorry to say—

They had no gift
For Mother that day,
Because they had lost
All of their pay.

Then Mother smiled,
"No gift did you bring?
The world is filled
With your gift of Spring!"

"You worked so hard,
And I know
You helped to make
The flowers grow.

Thank you for
The flowers in May,
Thank you for
My special day."

# Springtime Fun

# Flowers for Mom

Sung to: "Yankee Doodle"

Huff and Puff went off to work

To earn a little pay.

They needed money to buy a gift

For Mom on Mother's Day.

First they watered lots of lawns,

Then they washed some cars.

Next they soaked the elephants.

They worked so very hard.

Then they lost their money

And didn't know what to do.

So they sat and cried and cried,

"Boo-hoo, boo-hoo, boo-hoo!"

When at last the big day came,

The world was filled with flowers.

Mom was thrilled and so were they,

Thanks to their April Showers!

*Jean Warren*

## It Is Raining Everywhere

Sung to: "The Good Ship Lollipop"

It is raining everywhere,
It is raining, and we don't care.
Come on, let's play
While we watch the rain today.

It is raining on the hills,
It is raining on the daffodils.
Come on, let's play
While we watch the rain today.

It is raining on treetops,
It is raining on farmers' crops.
Come on, let's play
While we watch the rain today.

It is raining on the pond,
And the ducks keep swimming on.
Come on, let's play
While we watch the rain today.

*Jean Warren*

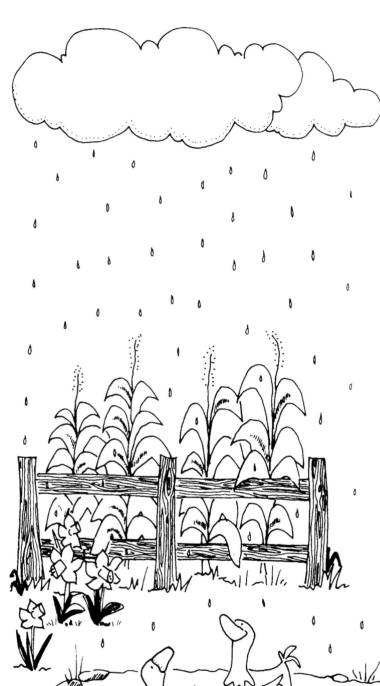

## In Our Springtime Garden
Sung to: "The Mulberry Bush"

What a lovely time of year,
Time of year, time of year.
What a lovely time of year
In our springtime garden.

See the flowers swing and sway,
Swing and sway, swing and sway.
See the flowers swing and sway
In our springtime garden.

*Jean Warren*

## A Little Flower Seed
Sung to: "Eensy, Weensy Spider"

A little flower seed
Burrowed deep within the ground.
Down came the rain,
And up grew a sprout.
Out came the sun
And a flower bloomed so bright,
All from a little seed,
What a lovely sight!

*Angela Wolfe*

## Happy Mother's Day to You

Sung to: "Mary Had a Little Lamb"

Happy Mother's Day to you,
Day to you, day to you.
Happy Mother's Day to you,
Oh, have a happy day!

This day was made just for you,
Just for you, just for you.
This day was made just for you,
Happy Mother's Day!

I have a kiss and a hug for you,
Hug for you, hug for you.
I have a kiss and a hug for you,
And I love you, too!

*Saundra Winnett*

## Thank You, Mom

Sung to: "London Bridge"

Thank you, Mom, for all your hugs,
All your hugs, all your hugs.
Thank you, Mom, for all your hugs.
They feel good to me.

Thank you, Mom, for all your kisses,
All your kisses, all your kisses.
Thank you, Mom, for all your kisses.
They feel good to me.

Thank you, Mom, for all your love,
All your love, all your love.
Thank you, Mom, for all your love.
It feels good to me.

*Becky Valenick*

# Making Rain

**1.**

**2.**

**3.**

**4.**

## *Make it rain inside!*

**1.** Fill a saucepan with water.

**2.** Heat the pan on a stove until steam starts forming a "cloud" above it.

**3.** Fill a metal pie plate with ice cubes. Hold the pie plate in the steam cloud.

**4.** Watch what happens when the steam comes in contact with the cool air from the pie pan. Drops of water will form and fall into the pot like rain.

### You Will Need
water • a saucepan • a metal pie plate • ice cubes

*Adult supervision or assistance may be required.*

# Rain Gauge

1.

2.

3.

## *Measure the rain with this homemade rain gauge!*

**1.** Hold a ruler against the side of a clear glass jar and use a permanent felt-tip marker to make a mark on the glass for each inch marking on the ruler.

**2.** Set your "rain gauge" outside in an area clear of trees and other things that could block rainfall.

**3.** After the next rainfall, check the gauge to see how much rain fell.

### For More Fun

• Leave the gauge outside to collect the rain that falls in a week or a month.

• Make a graph and keep track of the amount of rain that falls during each rainfall for a month.

### You Will Need
a clear glass jar • a permanent felt-tip marker • a ruler

# Rain Painting

3-4.

1-2.

5.

## *Use the rain as a paintbrush!*

**1.** Make sure it's raining!

**2.** Shake a few drops of food coloring onto a paper plate.

**3.** Hold your plate out an open window or take your plate outside.

**4.** Let the rain fall on your plate for a few moments.

**5.** Let your Rain Painting dry and then use it as a room decoration. Remember what fun you had on a rainy day!

## For More Fun

• Put drops of several different colors of food coloring on your plate and see what the rain does to the colors.

## You Will Need

a paper plate • food coloring

# Flower Garden

1.

2.

3.

4.

*Add some beauty to the world with your own flower garden!*

**1.** Fill a planter pot almost full with potting soil.

**2.** Place flower seeds an inch apart on the potting soil.

### You Will Need
a plastic or clay planter pot • potting soil • easy-to-grow flower seeds • water

**3.** Cover the seeds with about ¼ inch of soil.

**4.** Water the seeds, and place the planter pot outside in a sunny place.

**5.** Water the soil whenever it gets dry, and in a few weeks you will have your own flower garden.

# Plastic-Cup Terrarium

*Have fun growing plants without having to water them!*

**1.** Put a layer of pebbles and two or three inches of potting soil in a clear-plastic cup.

**2.** Plant a small plant in the soil.

**3.** Use an eyedropper to add a small amount of water to the soil.

**4.** Place a second plastic cup upside down on top of the first one and tape the cups together.

## For More Fun

• Set up a terrarium garden by making several terrariums with a different kind of small plant in each one. Place them side by side to make your garden.

### You Will Need

pebbles • potting soil • two clear-plastic cups • a small plant • eyedropper • water • tape

# Hand Print Garden Mural

## Put your hands to work "growing" this garden!

**1.** Pour each color of paint into a shallow container.

**2.** Tape a large white piece of butcher paper along a wall or spread it out on the floor or on a sidewalk outside.

### You Will Need

green, yellow, pink, blue, red, and white paint • shallow containers • a large white piece of butcher paper • tape • a paintbrush • felt-tip markers

**3.** Place your hands in the green paint, then make hand prints all across the bottom edge of the butcher paper to make a row of grass. Wash your hands.

**4.** Place your hands in the yellow paint. Make yellow hand prints wherever you want yellow flowers to be. Continue making flower prints with the other colors.

**5.** Use a paintbrush and the green paint to add stems to your flowers, then make green hand prints for leaves.

**6.** Make blue hand prints for birds. Use felt-tip markers to add bird faces and other details to your mural.

# Flower Jar

***Surprise Mom with this pretty gift!***

**1.** Place a small amount of clay in a baby food jar lid.

**2.** Push the stems of some dried flowers into the clay.

**3.** Place the jar over the dried flowers and twist it into the lid.

**4.** Tie a ribbon around the neck of the jar.

## You Will Need
clay • a baby food jar • small dried flowers • ribbon

## For More Fun

• Instead of dried flowers, use silk or paper flowers.

• Instead of dried flowers, use twigs or pieces of bushes.

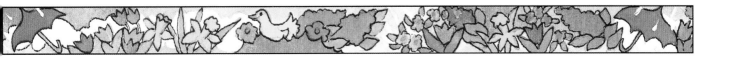

# Fancy Soaps

*Make these useful gifts anyone would love!*

**1.** In a large bowl, mix together Ivory Snow soap powder, water, and a few drops of food coloring until a doughlike mixture is formed.

**2.** Shape the soap dough into small balls and other shapes.

**3.** Place the soaps on waxed paper to dry for a few hours.

**4.** Place each dried soap (or several small soaps) in the middle of a tissue-paper square.

**5.** Pull up the ends of each tissue-paper square and tie ribbons around them.

**6.** Decorate the packages with stickers.

**7.** Give the Fancy Soaps as gifts.

## You Will Need

Ivory Snow soap powder • water • food coloring • a large bowl • spoon • waxed paper • tissue paper • ribbon • stickers

## For More Fun

• To make holiday shapes, mold your soap dough in cookie cutters. Let the soap dry in the cookie cutter and then pop it out.

# A Note to Parents and Teachers

The activities in this book have been written so that children in first, second, and third grade can follow most of the directions with minimal adult help.

The activities are also appropriate for 3- to 5-year-old children, who can easily do the suggested activities with your help.

You may wish to extend the story even further by discussing rain and all the ways it helps to make our world a better place. You could also use this story to discuss expectations and disappointments or low-cost gifts for people.

Learning about the life cycle of plants is exciting for young people. Why not set up a terrarium or plant a vegetable garden with your children?

Children learn so much better when they can express their ideas and feelings through age-appropriate activities. We know you'll enjoy seeing your children's eyes light up when you extend a story with related activities.